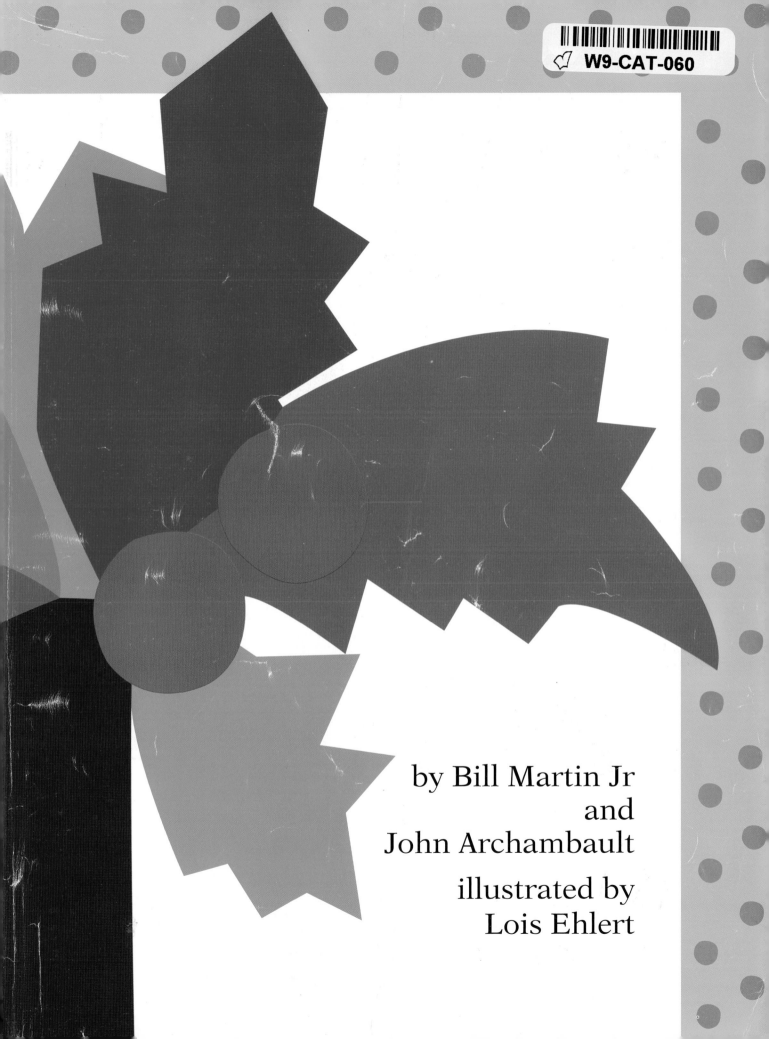

by Bill Martin Jr
and
John Archambault

illustrated by
Lois Ehlert

For Arie Alexander Archambault,
new baby boom boom
— J. A.

For Libby and Liza,
Helen and Morris
— L. E.

BEACH LANE BOOKS
An imprint of Simon & Schuster Children's Publishing Division
1230 Avenue of the Americas, New York, New York 10020
Text copyright © 1989 by Bill Martin Jr and John Archambault
Illustrations copyright © 1989 by Lois Ehlert
Preface copyright © 2009 by Lois Ehlert and John Archambault
Poster illustration copyright © 2009 by Lois Ehlert
All rights reserved, including the right of reproduction in whole or in part in any form.
BEACH LANE BOOKS is a trademark of Simon & Schuster, Inc.
Manufactured in the United States of America 0613 LAK
8 10 9 7
Library of Congress Cataloging-in-Publication Data
Martin, Bill, 1916–2004.
Chicka chicka boom boom : anniversary edition / Bill Martin Jr and John Archambault ;
illustrated by Lois Ehlert. — 1st ed.
p. cm.
Summary: An alphabet rhyme/chant that relates what happens when the whole alphabet
tries to climb a coconut tree.
ISBN: 978-1-4169-9091-8 (alk. paper)
[1. Stories in rhyme. 2. Alphabet—Fiction.]
I. Archambault, John. II. Ehlert, Lois, ill. III. Title.
PZ8.3.M418Ch 2009
[E]—dc22   2009000626

A Bit of **Chicka** History

More than twenty-five years ago, Bill Martin Jr and I were at a hotel in San Francisco, conducting a workshop for teachers on the power of poetry and predictable text for early readers. A man introduced himself, explaining that he hadn't learned to read until the fifth grade, when his class came up with a lively cheer that began with "Chigga Chigga whole potata, half past alligata, bim bam bulligata." By connecting the rhythm and sounds with the letters he saw written on the chalkboard, he finally began to read.

I couldn't get that story and that cheer out of my head, and as I said the cheer over and over to my six-month-old son, it evolved—in that wonderful way that things often do when you repeat them a lot to your baby—into "Chicka Chicka Boom Boom."

Around that time, Bill and I got the idea to write an alphabet book together, and "Chicka Chicka Boom Boom"—plus the palm tree outside my California windows— became the center of the piece. Bill and I ping-ponged back and forth over the phone, reciting and rewriting the book literally dozens of times. "John, what happens after the letters climb up the tree?" Bill asked one day. Another day he called and said, "John, I've got one. How about black-eyed P?" That led to my favorite: "loose-tooth T!" The traffic jams I'd see of parents picking up their children when school let out each day inspired the second half of the book. Naturally, the lowercase letters became the children and the capital letters the "mamas and papas and uncles and aunts." Bill and I had a blast working together. I used to laugh and say, "Can you believe two grown men would play with the alphabet for weeks . . . and actually have fun doing it?!"

I am blessed to have had Bill Martin Jr as a mentor and a friend, and I am honored to have worked with him for over a decade—a joyous collaboration that produced more than a dozen books. I will never forget his marvelous ear for language and his face-lit grin when he would turn to me and say, "John, that's it! That's a book!"

—John Archambault

When I first read the *Chicka* text, I thought: I can do a butterfly, a squirrel, a fish, or a cat, but letters climbing up a coconut tree? I can't do that! I read the words over again. I thought it sounded like the letters of the alphabet were having a party in that coconut tree. I began cutting out the letters from colored paper with my scissors, and then I made a polka-dot border for a stage. Soon *Chicka* and I were dancing together, words and pictures moving in a festive rhythm that still gets me tapping my toes, even after all these years!

—Lois Ehlert

A told **B**,
and **B** told **C**,
"I'll meet you at the top
of the coconut tree."

"Whee!" said **D**
to **E F G**.
"I'll beat you to the top
of the coconut tree."

Chicka chicka boom boom!
Will there be enough room?
Here comes **H**
up the coconut tree,

and **I** and **J**
and tag-along **K**,
all on their way
up the coconut tree.

Chicka chicka boom boom!
Will there be enough room?
Look who's coming!
L M N O P!

And **Q R S**!

And **T U V**!

Still more—**W**!
And **X Y Z**!

The whole alphabet
up the—Oh, no!

Chicka chicka…
BOOM! BOOM!

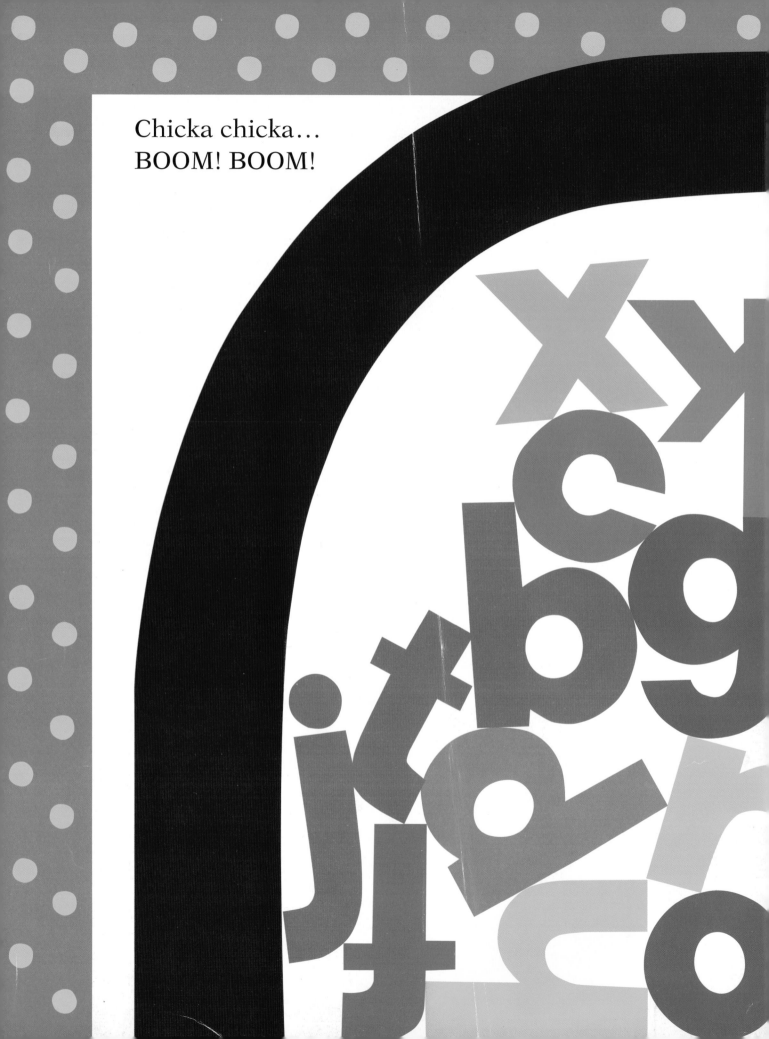

Skit skat skoodle doot.
Flip flop flee.
Everybody running to the coconut tree.
Mamas and papas
and uncles and aunts
hug their little dears,
then dust their pants.

"Help us up,"
cried **A B C**.

Next from the pileup
skinned-knee **D**
and stubbed-toe **E**
and patched-up **F**.
Then comes **G**
all out of breath.

M is looped.
N is stooped.
O is twisted alley-oop.
Skit skat skoodle doot.
Flip flop flee.

Look who's coming!
It's black-eyed **P**,
Q R S,
and loose-tooth **T**.

Then **U** **V** **W**
wiggle-jiggle free.

Last to come
X Y Z.
And the sun goes down
on the coconut tree...

But—
chicka chicka boom boom!
Look, there's a full moon.